Louie's Search

EZRA JACK KEATS

FOUR WINDS PRESS   NEW YORK

Four Winds Press
Macmillan Publishing Company
866 Third Avenue, New York, NY 10022
Collier Macmillan Canada, Inc.

Printed in the United States of America
Library of Congress Catalog Card Number: 80-10176
First Edition
10 9 8 7 6 5 4 3

LIBRARY OF CONGRESS CATALOGING IN PUBLICATION DATA

Keats, Ezra Jack.
   Louie's search.

   Summary: Louie goes out looking for a new father and instead
finds a music box which he is accused of stealing. Or is that all he
finds?
   [1. Remarriage—Fiction]   I. Title.
PZ7.K2253Lr   [E]   80-10176   ISBN 0-02-749700-3

To Dean Engel

"What kind of neighborhood is this?"
thought Louie.
"Nobody notices a kid around here."
Louie put on some funny things
and took a walk.
Maybe someone would notice him—
someone he'd like for a father.

Louie passed quite a few people.
He looked them over,
and walked on.

People were going up and down,
and in and out.
He wanted to say something to them,
but they were too busy.

Louie walked backward,
still looking at them.
He bumped into a man
carrying a big cake.

"Watch where you're going!"
the man yelled.
Louie turned around
and walked forward.

He saw a truck piled high with old furniture.

As he got closer, something fell off.

Louie picked it up to put it back.

It began to play music!

The man in the truck turned around.

He looked terrible!

"Hey!" he yelled. "What are you doing with that?"

Louie was so scared, he couldn't speak.

The man jumped off the truck, and chased Louie.
"Come back, you little crook!" he bellowed.

Louie fell!

The man stared down at him.

"You stole it!" he shouted. "Where do you live?"

"No, I didn't steal it," Louie cried. "Ow! Ow! My foot!"

Louie pointed to where he lived.

They went into his house.

"Louie! What happened?" his mother gasped. "And who are you?"

"Your son's a crook!"

"What? IMPOSSIBLE! He's the best boy in the world!"

"Ow! Ow! He broke my foot!" Louie cried.

"Really? You're still standing on it— and what's that music I hear?"

Louie saw that he was still holding the box.

He dropped it.

BANG! It stopped playing.

"Now you broke my beautiful music maker!" the man boomed.

"You'll pay for this!"

The house got quiet.

"WELL, WHAT ARE YOU GOING TO DO?" the man shouted, shaking his fists in the air.

The whole room shook. The music box began to play.

The man looked around, surprised.
"Err—ya know what? That thing never
played like that for me before,"
said the man.

"See? And you blamed Louie," his mother said.

"If I know him, he was only trying to put it back."

Louie nodded.

"Well—in that case—I'm sorry," the man mumbled.

He picked up the box and started to leave.

Then he turned around and said,

"Since it plays so good for you, Louie,

why don't you keep it? Here's the windup key."

Louie jumped up and down.

His foot felt fine.

"By the way," said the man, "my name's Barney,"
and he bowed a little.

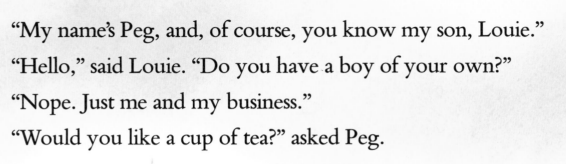

"My name's Peg, and, of course, you know my son, Louie."

"Hello," said Louie. "Do you have a boy of your own?"

"Nope. Just me and my business."

"Would you like a cup of tea?" asked Peg.

A few days later Barney returned.

He took them in his truck to the waterfront.

Barney knew just about everybody!

The tugboat men gave them a ride on their boat.

Barney visited Louie and Peg again and again.

Then, one Sunday, at the end of summer...

Barney and Peg got married!
They had a wonderful wedding.
And all their friends and neighbors came.